To do LIST

1. ~~EAT porridge~~
2. ~~Fix CHAIR~~
3. ~~Eat More porridge~~
4. Make Bed
5. EAT even MoRE porridge
6. go FoR a nice Big WALK.

For **ELLiot**
the
newest
Little
BEAR
in
TOWN

JUMBO OATS

honey

ISBN 978-1-338-14818-3

Copyright © 2011 by Leigh Hodgkinson. All rights reserved. Published by Scholastic Inc., 557 Broadway, New York, NY 10012, by arrangement with Nosy Crow, an imprint of Candlewick Press. SCHOLASTIC and associated logos are trademarks and/or registered trademarks of Scholastic Inc.

12 11 10 9 8 7 6 5 4 3 2 1   16 17 18 19 20 21

Printed in the U.S.A.   40

First Scholastic printing, October 2016

This book was typeset in Bodoni Classic HD. The illustrations were done in mixed media.

Goldilocks
AND JUST ONE BEAR

Leigh HODGKINSON

SCHOLASTIC INC.

Once upon a time, there was this bear.

One minute, he was strolling in the woods, all happy-go-lucky. . . .

The next minute, he didn't have a crumb-of-a-clue where he was.

He was one **COMPLETELY** lost bear.

The bear didn't much like this place.
Too many BRIGHT Lights and not enough twigs.

Too much loud HONKING and BEEPING
and not NEARLY enough owl hooting.

The bear was also a teeny bit scared,
and his furry legs were slightly WOBBLY.

"Maybe the thing to do," said the bear, looking
around, "is to pop into Snooty Towers and get
away from this TERRIBLE racket."

But the revolving door at Snooty Towers made the bear dizzy,
and being dizzy with woBBLY legs was bad news.

What the bear needed
was a little rest.

A little rest
somewhere would
DEFINITELY
make things right.

18th floor

17th floor

16th floor

15th floor

14th floor

The bear peeked through a door and thought how **VERY** pleasant it was up here.

"Not nasty and **NOISY** like down there," said the bear. "Just the place for a little rest."

All that **whooSHY** traveling was certainly a hungry business, so before his little rest, a little porridge seemed like a good idea. . . .

THIS porridge is a bit on the D R Y side, but it is better than nothing.

Now the bear was ready for his little rest.

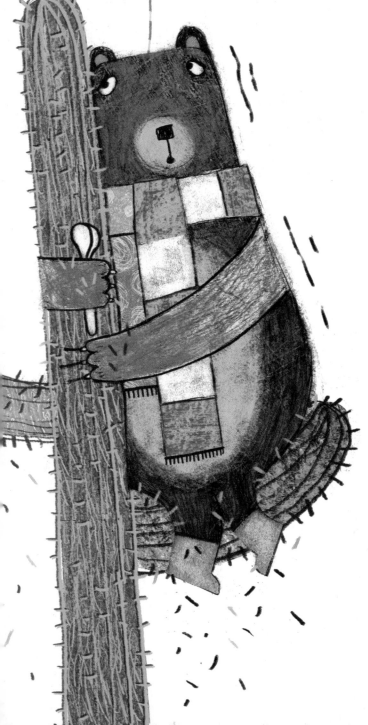

THIS chair is **JUST** right!

A little rest is nice, but what the bear needed
to really feel like himself again was a good
old-fashioned nap in a comfy bed.

THIS bed is too *frothy*.

THIS bed is too *pink*.

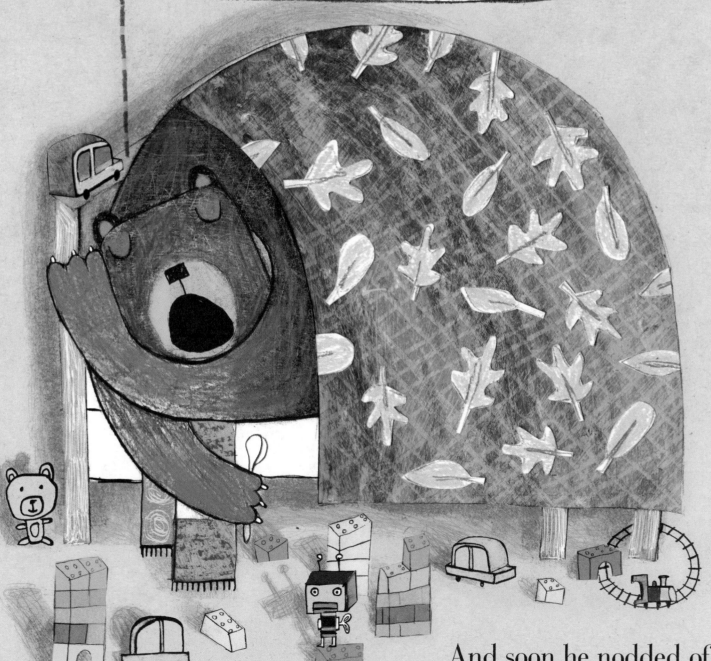

THIS bed is **just** right!

And soon he nodded off.

The bear dreamed of

CRUNCHING

through leaves.

The bear dreamed of **puttering** around in his slippers.

The bear dreamed of

a voice shouting very, VERY LOUDLY.

"**SOMEBODY** has been eating from my fishbowl!" said the daddy person.

"Somebody has been eating my dear little Pumpkin's kitty nibbles!" said the mommy person.

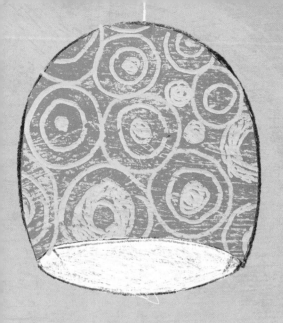

Unfortunately,
the bear was not
dreaming at all.
He was

WIDE AWAKE

and back in real life again.

"And somebody
has been eating
my toast," said
the little person.
"And they've
eaten it all up!"

"SOMEBODY has SQUISHED my cactus!" said the daddy person.

"**Somebody** has **UPSET** my dear little Pumpkin!" said the mommy person.

"And **SOMEBODY** has **POPPED** my beanbag chair!" said the little person.

"SOMEBODY has been sleeping in my bath!" said the daddy person.

"Somebody has been sleeping in my bed!" said the mommy person.

"Shhhhh!" whispered the little person.
"I think that **somebody** is sleeping in MY bed right now!"

The bear peeked from under the covers to see a daddy person, a mommy person, and a little person standing right there.

The bear thought that the mommy person looked ever so slightly familiar. And the mommy person thought that . . .

gobbling other people's breakfast,

BREAKING other people's stuff,

and **snoozing** in other people's beds

seemed ever so slightly familiar, too. And it was!

"Baby Bear?"
said the
mommy person.

"Goldilocks?" said the bear.

They hadn't seen each other in ages!
"Porridge?" asked Goldilocks.
The bear nodded.
So Goldilocks cooked up a BIG bowl
and plunked it in front of him.

It was not too HOT.

It was not too COLD.

It was JUST right.

It made the bear almost forget about that once-upon-a-time when

Goldilocks had behaved so BADLY.

THIS little bear would never DREAM of doing

ANYTHING

like that.

And although it had been good
to see Goldilocks living so *happily ever after*
with those C H A R M I N G people,
the bear decided it was time to go back
home to the woods.